Practicing Mindfulness

Emma Lou the Yorkie Poo's Activity and Coloring Book for Kids

Kim Larkins, LCSW

Loving Healing Press
Ann Arbor, MI

Practicing Mindfulness: Emma Lou the Yorkie Poo's Activity and Coloring Book for Kids

Learn more at www.KimLarkins.Net

ISBN 978-1-61599-698-8 paperback
ISBN 978-1-61599-699-5 hardcover

Published by
Loving Healing Press
5145 Pontiac Trail
Ann Arbor, MI 48105

www.LHPress.com   Tollfree 888-761-6268
info@LHPress.com   FAX 734-663-6861

Distributed by Ingram Book Groop (USA/CAN/UK/Australia)

Contents

Introduction

Hi, everybody! Emma Lou the Yorkie Poo here with my two friends, Pearl and Gigi the Gentle Ginormous Giraffe, to tell you about mindfulness. This activity book is to help you to remember to be mindful and give you some fun things to do at the same time! But first, Gigi would like to explain how we will begin.

Hi, boys and girls, I hope you enjoy this activity book. Mindfulness is all about paying attention to what is going on right now. That means we are in the present moment. Right now, you are reading (or listening) to this book. You are in the present moment! When we stay in the present moment, we notice what is going on around us, or practicing being mindful. Can you draw a picture on the next page of you in the present moment?

Picture of me in the present moment: *What am I doing right now?*

How to Focus on Your Breath

We will learn many things in this activity book. Right now, we will learn to focus on our breath. First, sit up tall, like Pearl, Emma Lou and our friend, Patrick. Gently close your eyes or look down at my floor. I want you to breathe in and out. You may notice three spots in your body. First try to notice your breath in your belly. Try that for about 15 seconds (if you don't have someone to time you, no worries, just take a guess.) Now move your attention to your chest or heart area. See if you can notice your breathing there for 15 seconds. Now try and feel your breath coming in and out of your nose. You may want to hold your hand in front of your face for this part.

When you are finished, take a minute to think where in your body it was easiest to focus on your breath. Was it your nose? Your chest or heart? Your belly? That is how we hold our attention in place while we breathe. Just like an anchor keeps a boat from floating away, feeling your breath in your body will help keep your attention from floating away.

1) Nose

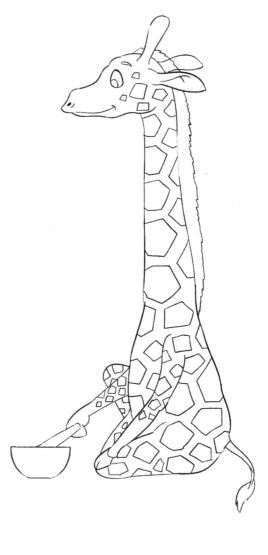

2) Chest

3) Belly

Circle and Color Your Anchor

Mindful Listening

Next we will practice mindful listening. Please sit tall and discover how still and quiet you can be. When you are still and quiet, listen to all the sounds around you for about one minute.

Make a list of as many sounds you heard when you were still and quiet.

1.

2.

3.

4.

5.

6.

7.

8.

9.

10.

Exploring the Attitude of Gratitude

Gigi said, "Gather around, everyone. A very important piece of mindfulness is in your heart. When we are mindful, we try to fill our hearts with joy and gratitude. Do you know what gratitude means?"

"I know, I know!" said Pearl as she twirled in the air. "It's when you are thankful for something. I am thankful, or grateful, that I have so many friends and you are all here today!"

"That's right, Pearl!" Gigi said. "Who else can tell me something that gives them joy in their hearts?"

"I am grateful for my toys and sharing them with my friends," said Katie the Kangaroo.

"I am grateful for music," said Beatrice Butterfly. "Music fills my heart with joy."

"I am grateful for the sunshine on my face when I run in the fields and play," shared Henry the Horse.

"And I am grateful for my teachers and my school," said Emma Lou. "I really missed them when we had to stay and learn at home."

"Those are super things you all shared!" said Gigi.

List 10 things that give you a feeling of gratitude.

1.

2.

3.

4.

5.

6.

7.

8.

9.

10.

What's Going on in YOUR Body?

Let's talk about body sensations!" Gigi said next. "When we are mindful, we need to know what we feel in our body. Then we can know what we feel in our mind."

"I don't understand, Gigi," said Pearl.

"Well," said Gigi, "when you are angry, what do you feel in your body?"

"I know the answer to that!" said Abigail the Antelope. "Sometimes when I feel angry my face gets red and hot and my body shakes all over."

"Hot and shaky are body sensations, Abigail! What are some others?"

"When I am nervous, I feel like I have butterflies in my belly and I feel my heart pounding in my chest," said Wyatt the Wallaby.

"That's silly," said Beatrice Butterfly. "You feel me in your belly?"

Emma Lou said, "I notice that, too, because I worry a lot. My head also hurts when I worry."

"Those are all body sensations," said Gigi, "and they can help us know when we need to calm our mind and body."

"That's right," said Emma Lou. "You taught me, Gigi, to breathe when I notice that I am worrying. My body tells me when to start breathing in and out."

"You are all so smart and brave to talk about how you are feeling," said Gigi.

10

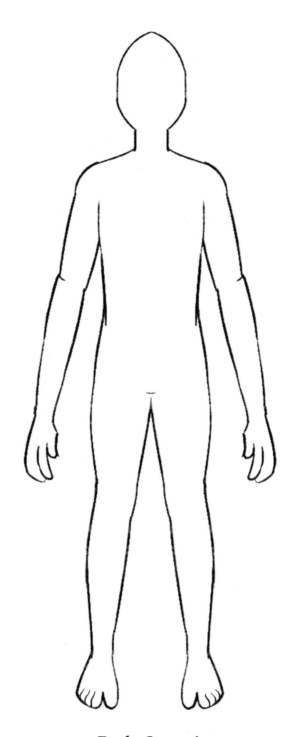

Body Sensations

Choose an emotion: worried, happy, sad, angry, bored, or choose something else.

Label the sensation where you feel it in your body: hot, cold, shaky, itchy, pounding, "butterflies," or choose something else.

MY EMOTION IS_____

The Importance of Being Present

"We are going to talk more about the present moment and how sometimes our minds wander away from what we are doing," Gigi said.

"Sometimes our minds wander to the past or to the future, or something that hasn't happened yet. Pearl, can you give an example of when your mind wanders to the future?"

"I'm always wondering when Beatrice and the Monarchs are coming to visit. I love twirling with them so much!" answered Pearl.

"That's a great example. It might be something we want to do or might be doing in the future!"

"I can think of something from the past," said Emma Lou. "Sometimes I think about how I used to worry all the time and wish I had known about breathing before."

"That's okay, Emma Lou. Now you know and when you notice your mind wandering to the past, you can come back to the present moment and think about what you are doing right now," said Gigi.

"When we are mindful, we stay in the present moment."

1

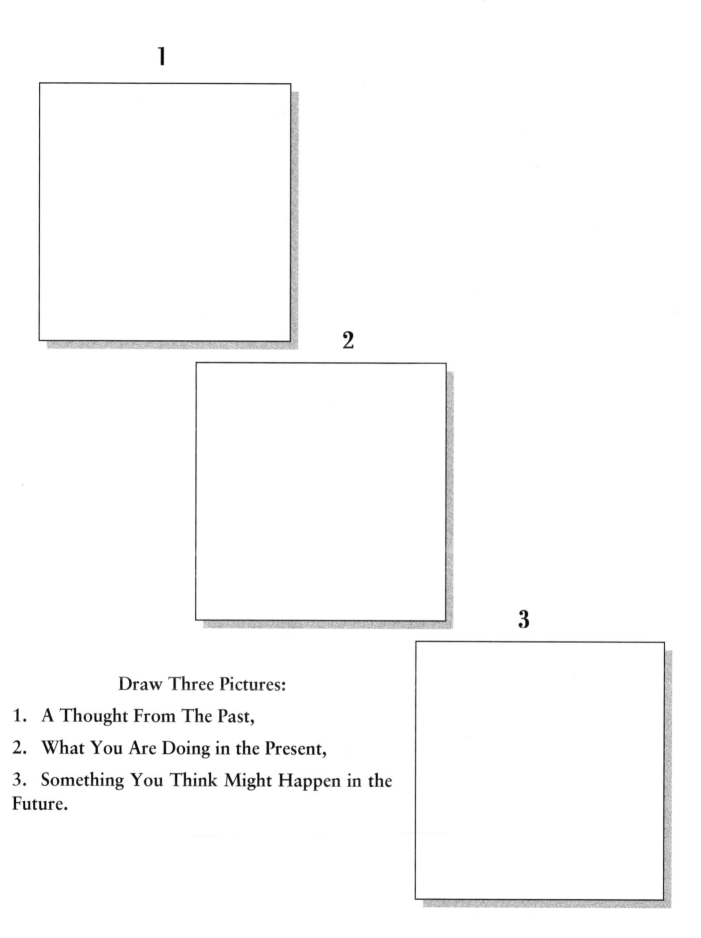

2

3

Draw Three Pictures:

1. A Thought From The Past,

2. What You Are Doing in the Present,

3. Something You Think Might Happen in the Future.

Fill Your Heart with Generosity

Hello, friends," Gigi said next, "I want to share something else about mindfulness that can bring joy to our hearts. We will talk about generosity."

"That's easy," said Pearl, "generosity is when you give someone a gift. I am going to a birthday party and I am buying a present for my friend."

"That's one way we can show generosity, Pearl, but there are other ways to be generous that you can't buy at the store. Does anyone know some of those ways?" asked Gigi.

Melissa the Musical Monarch explained, "I feel generous when I share my music with you."

"And we love your music, Melissa!" Caleb shouted.

"I use my courage to help others when they are in trouble," said Caleb. "Is that being generous, Gigi?"

"It sure is! Any time we help others, we are showing generosity," noted Gigi.

Lucy the Llama shared, "I give my mama lots of hugs and smiles. I am very generous with my hugs!"

Jenny the Jaguar seemed a little sad today. She said, "Pearl always helps by talking to me when I feel sad. I think she is a generous, kind and caring listener."

"These all fill my heart with joy!" said Emma Lou. "Generosity makes me feel happy!"

What can you put in the box as your gift of generosity? Remember to put words in the gift box that we can't buy at the store.

Mindfulness Word Search

Here are lots of letters, and some words below them. Find the words!

```
P  R  K  J  E  F  G  N  D  M  E
R  O  P  I  Q  H  E  F  I  J  C
E  H  I  J  N  T  T  N  O  P  I
S  C  D  E  S  D  D  A  B  C  T
E  N  O  I  J  F  N  O  E  F  O
N  A  L  M  U  X  Y  E  F  R  N
T  U  V  L  M  N  O  P  S  U  B
C  D  E  M  O  T  I  O  N  S  T
S  T  H  G  U  O  H  T  P  Q  A
```

Keywords to find in the puzzle are below:

BREATHE	THOUGHTS	ANCHOR
MINDFUL	EMOTIONS	KINDNESS
PRESENT	NOTICE	LISTEN

Hint #1: words can go up, down, left, right, and diagonal. They can also go forwards or backwards!

Hint #2: if you need help, you can check the answer key in the back of the book

Help Emma Lou and Pearl find Gigi's House

Emma Lou is feeling particularly sad and worried today. She and Pearl are playing in the dog park, but Emma Lou can't get her mind off her worries. She needs help.

"We can go visit Gigi the Ginormous Giraffe and she can give you some advice, Emma Lou!" said Pearl. She was very excited to help her friend and knew just the place to go.

"That's a great idea, Pearl," Emma Lou said. She had forgotten that Gigi was very good at helping others understand their feelings and had told Emma Lou to come and visit any time she needed help.

It's always a good idea to have someone you trust who can help you with your feelings when you're not sure what to do.

Can you help Emma Lou and Pearl find their way to Gigi's house? Follow the maze and when you get to Gigi's, don't forget to ask for help.

Feelings Crossword Puzzle

Follow the clues on the next page to fill the boxes!

Crossword Clues

Instructions: find another word that starts with the same letter as the animal. The word will also fill in the blank in the sentence:

Down

1. Patrick the Pig calms his mind and body when he breathes. He feels_____

2. Scarlet and Sophia Swans have fun when they laugh and twirl. They are _____ swans.

3. Finn the Fox is scared of the dark. He feels_____

8. Rudy the Reindeer feels calm and rested after a long day. Rudy does his breathing to _____

Across

4. Thomas the Turtle is grateful he has nice friends. Thomas is _____ for his friends.

5. Davis the Dog is overjoyed when he dances with his friends. He is _____ they come to visit

6. Isabel the Iguana is annoyed when she's hungry and tired. Isabel feels _____

7. Caleb the Cat is brave and strong. Caleb is a _____ cat.

9. Abigail the Antelope's face gets bright red and her heart starts to pound. Sometimes, we all get _____

10. Katie the Kangaroo says nice things to her friends. Katie is a _____ Kangaroo

Hint: if you need help, see the answer key at the very back of this book!

The Importance of Kindness and Caring

Gigi and Katie the Kangaroo want to remind you that it's important to be kind and caring. Being kind to others is important, but it's also important to be kind to yourself. We feel joy in our hearts when we are kind to ourselves and others.

"Think of someone you see every day that you think might need some extra love and joy today," said Gigi. "Close your eyes or look down at the grass and repeat after me (pause to repeat each line):

"I wish you peace,"

"I wish you joy,"

"I wish you health,"

"I wish you love."

Now open your eyes and give yourself a big hug!

Draw a picture of who you sent kindness and caring

Be Kind to Yourself Too!

"Do you remember I said it's important to also be kind to yourself?" asked Gigi. "I want to remind you that you are like rays of sunshine! You are bright and shine in so many ways. Feel proud of who you are and share your love and kindness with others."

"I like that I can draw," said Finn the Fox.

Emma Lou added, "I like to share my toys!"

"And I love to help my friends!" Pearl added.

"Those are all great things," said Zarah the Zebra. "I love my fancy stripes! You all have so many special things about you!"

Fill the rays with all the special things about you!

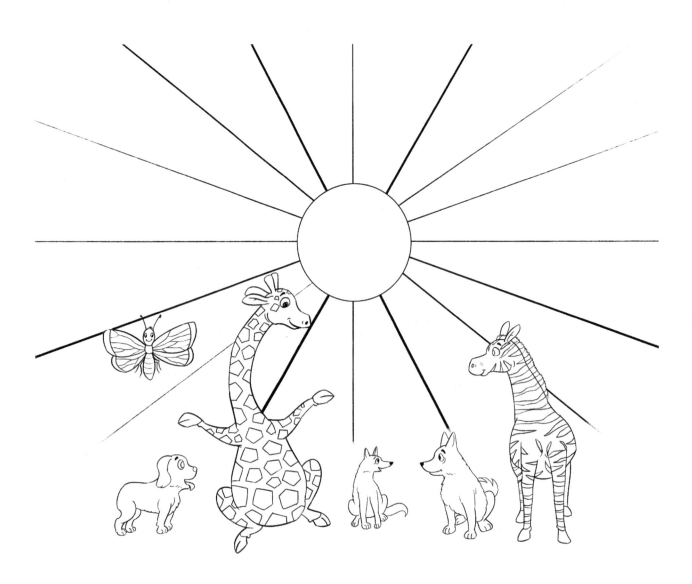

Dance Like Nobody Is Watching

"Look! It's Davis the Dog!" Emma Lou was so excited to see her dancing friend.

"Let's do some mindful movement," said Davis. "Turn on some music and move your body!"

"Do you remember what sensations are?" Davis asked.

"Sure, I do," said Pearl. "Sensations are what you feel in your body. When I dance my heart starts to pound faster, my legs get a little shaky and my head feels dizzy if I spin too fast."

"You're right, Pearl. Those are all sensations you feel in your body," said Davis.

Davis, Emma Lou and Pearl feel delighted when they dance. While YOU are dancing, notice how your body moves and what sensations you feel.

List 3 sensations you noticed:

1._____

2._____

3._____

Breathing in the Calm

"Now we are going to slow down and practice another way to calm our bodies while we breathe. Do you remember when we danced under the stars and the moon? We are going to use this star to practice breathing in and out. Use your paws to trace around the star's points and breathe in on one side and out on the other. Trace all the way around the star and notice how you feel when you are finished. You can also color the star. What color is your star?"

"S.T.A.R. stands for Smile, Take a deep breath And Relax. Taking three deep belly breaths helps to calm the fight, flight, or freeze response in the body."

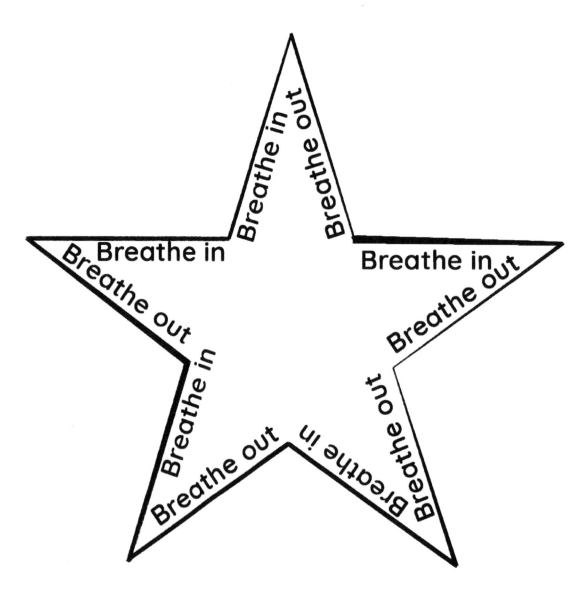

Do You Remember?

See how many things you can remember from this book by filling the bubbles
with your thoughts about mindfulness

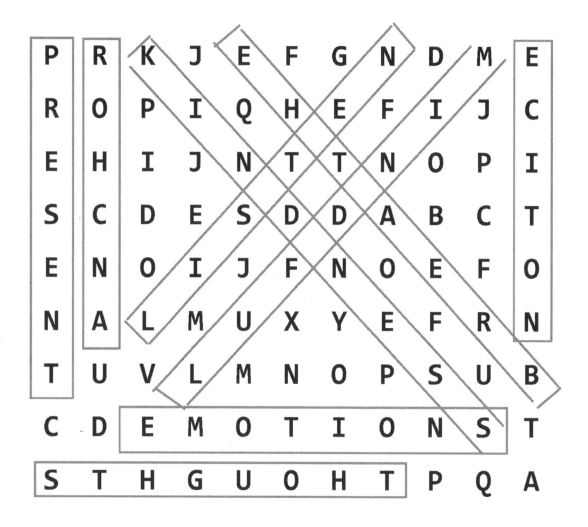

Crossword Key
(if you need help)

	¹p								²s
	e								i
³f	⁴t	h	a	n	k	f	u	l	
r	c								l
⁵d	e	l	i	g	h	t	e	d	y
g	f								
h	u								
⁶i	r	r	i	t	a	t	e	d	l
e									
n									
⁷c	o	u	⁸r	a	g	e	o	u	s
e			d						
l									
⁹a	n	g	r	y					
x									
e									
¹⁰k	i	n	d						

About the Author

Kim Larkins is a Licensed Clinical Social Worker in private practice. For the past thirty years, Kim has dedicated her career working with children and families in the mental health and human services field.

She currently spends part of her practice in a rural educational setting developing mindfulness skills with students and enhancing social emotional development through direct service.

Kim has a Master of Social Work degree from the University of Maine. She is also licensed in Maine where she works and lives. You can contact her by:

- email at kimlarkinslcsw@gmail.com
- Facebook @kim.larkins.author

Notes

The adventure begins with *Breathing in the Calm*!

Meet Emma Lou, the Yorkie Poo—a little dog with big worries. She loves playing with her best friend, Pearl, but Pearl doesn't always pay attention to Emma Lou's worries. With the help of some new friends, Caleb the Calico cat, Patrick the pig and Gigi the ginormous giraffe, Emma Lou and Pearl begin to learn a new technique to calm their minds and bodies. Parents, educators, counselors - and especially children - can benefit from Emma Lou and her friends' curious adventure to a mindful experience.

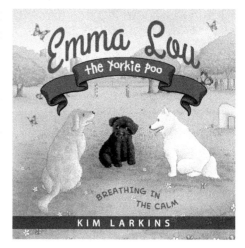

Readers will:

- Learn how to help a child that worries

- Teach children a simple technique to practice mindfulness

- Support your child's emotional growth through experiencing a delightful adventure

"*Emma Lou the Yorkie Poo: Breathing in the Calm* is a playful approach to real concerns that kids have on a daily basis. Kim uses relatable animal characters to bring to light concerns that impact children everywhere - along with a great strategy to help!"

-- Marie Robinson, M.Ed., principal, pre-K to 12

"For over 20 years, I have noted our children experiencing increasing levels of joy-blocking anxiety. In this whimsical and engaging story, Kim has created a very useful therapeutic tool. She captured the essence of a hopeful way out that children can readily identify with and rapidly incorporate, just like Emma Lou did!"

-- John Pasquarelli, LCSW, LADC

"Kim is a warm, kind and compassionate social worker dedicated to improving the lives of others. Her book is an easy read for children to learn about managing anxiety and contains techniques that can be applied right away."

-- Gwen M. Ackley, LCSW

"With excessive exposure to flashing changing screens, children are having a hard time settling their brains. Their thinking is fragmented and their focus is fractured. In *Emma Lou the Yorkie Poo: Breathing In The Calm*, Kim Larkins cleverly and creatively invites children into an animal-friendly storyline of learning how to calm themselves. Although Larkins addresses worry, *Emma Lou* is a valuable tool for releasing stress throughout the nervous system, induced from screen stimulation."

-- Holli Kenley, author of Power Down & Parent Up

From Loving Healing Press
www.LHPress.com

Discover a World of Feelings with Emma Lou the Yorkie Poo

Emma Lou and Pearl return with some old and new friends in *Emma Lou the Yorkie Poo: Alphabet, Feelings and Friends*. Join them as they experience, through a collection of whimsical rhymes, a wide range of emotions. From A to Z, Emma Lou and Pearl invite children to bring emotions to life and provide reassurance that all feelings are expected and accepted.

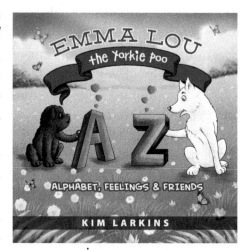

To cope with our changing world during this vulnerable time in our history, children now more than ever need to feel free to express their fears, worries and joys. *Alphabet, Feelings and Friends* is a resource for parents, educators and mental health workers to assist children in developing meaningful discussions and insight into their present experiences.

"In a short period of time, readers--and the adults who care for them--can review the brightly colored pages of this alphabet book. This A-Z guide provides rich examples of social and emotional growth experiences for children that can be utilized at home, in the classroom or at therapy spaces."
-- Theresa Fraser, CYC-P, CPT-S, RP, MA, RTC, author of *We're Not All the Same, But We're Family*

"Kim Larkins has written a sweet book that introduces young children to 26 emotions that align with each letter of the alphabet. She uses animal characters, rhymes and fanciful pictures as the vehicle for describing that mindful activities can influence how one feels. "
-- Laurie Zelinger, PhD, ABPP, RPT-S, board certified psychologist and author, former director: New York Association for Play Therapy

"With delightful illustrations and lovely rhymes, this book is a must for any educator, parent or caregiver who wants to help children learn about and manage their emotions. Don't miss this opportunity to journey through the alphabet with delightful pups Emma Lou and Pearl and discover a little mindfulness too! "
-- Kellie Doyle Bailey, MA CCC-SLP, MMT/SELI, author of *Some Days I Flip My Lid, Some Nights I Flip My Lid - Learning to be Calm Cool Kids.*

From Loving Healing Press
www.LHPress.com

CPSIA information can be obtained
at www.ICGtesting.com
Printed in the USA
JSHW060208081022
31443JS00005B/34

9 781615 996988